# JENNY
# CAN'T
# READ

# JENNY CAN'T READ

Kevin Clarke and Demi Dutton

authorHOUSE®

AuthorHouse™
1663 Liberty Drive
Bloomington, IN 47403
www.authorhouse.com
Phone: 1-800-839-8640

Published by AuthorHouse    08/07/2012

ISBN: 978-1-4772-1909-6 (sc)
ISBN: 978-1-4772-1908-9 (e)

# 1

## I HATE SCHOOL

Until I was ten my life was quite
normal, apart from one thing. I lived
with my mum and dad. My Nan lived
in the next street and my best friend
Kirsty lived three doors away. She was
the same age as me but she went to

a different school because her mum worked there as a teaching assistant.

The one thing about me that wasn't normal was that I couldn't read. I didn't know about Dyslexia then. I thought it was because I was stupid. I thought that there was something wrong with me. I couldn't do things that other children could do. I used to think, "Why me?"

I can remember feeling sad or upset for a lot of the time. I worried a lot and I dreaded some lessons. I was also quite lonely because I was shy and nervous and didn't have any friends in my class. I used to stand on my own in the yard. Sometimes the other girls in my class would have sleepovers at each other's houses, but I never got invited. I was secretly glad because I don't think I would have enjoyed them. I would have been too worried.

I hated going to school. I was always worried that I might be asked to read something and would feel ashamed when I couldn't do it. I used to worry a lot. I would lie in bed thinking all sorts of things. "I'll never pass any exams. I'll never get a job when I'm older. When I go to secondary school other children will skit me."

I often used to pretend that I was sick. I was a good actress and sometimes the school would ring my mum and ask her to come and get me because I wasn't well. My mum used to get really annoyed and say that there was nothing wrong with me. She even told the school that I was putting it on.

I really hated being in Year 5. We had a teacher Mrs. Old who was very strict. She shouted a lot and never smiled. I could tell that she didn't like me, because she used to say things to me that made me really upset. Once she made me feel really ashamed in front of the whole class. She said to me in a narky voice, "I know you can't read, and do you know why? It's because you don't try hard enough. Other children find it difficult to learn to read but they practice and practice and practice. But you can't be bothered! . . . . You're lazy! . . . . You give up too easily! And then you expect me to spend half my time helping you. You can think again young lady!"

I can remember that I couldn't stop sobbing for ages. It was so unfair. She didn't know how hard I had tried.

I have lots of terrible memories from Year 5. Mrs. Old would keep children in at playtime if they hadn't finished their work. I was always being kept in. Once the boy who sat next to me let me copy his work to try and help me. Mrs. Old went mad and said that I was a cheat and kept me in at lunchtime as well.

The thing I dreaded most was the spelling test which we had every Monday. Mrs. Old would give us twenty spellings to learn over the week-end. We were tested on Monday morning in school. She would read out all the scores. A few of the children would get them all right and were given a star. Most of the others would get most of them right and three of us used to only get a few right. She would read out all the scores and it always finished with her saying, "and Jenny Button got three out of twenty". Sometimes it might be two or four but I was always worse than everyone else.

Mrs. Old would say. "Some teachers don't read out the low scores, but I do, because it will make those children make more effort. Anyone can remember a spelling if they go over it often enough."

If only she knew that I did go over and over them, but the next day I had forgotten them.

Once I decided to cheat. I wrote the words down on a bit of paper and hid the paper under my book. I got nearly all the spellings right. When Mrs. Old was reading out the scores she didn't say well done. She just said. "This shows that for once you've made an effort to learn them. You could have done that in the first place. I've been right about you all along". One of the girls in the class, Amy Connor smiled at me and whispered "Well done, Jenny".

If only she knew how much that meant.

I now had a problem. I didn't like being a cheat. I felt really bad about it. I only did it because I couldn't stand it when the results were read out and everyone looked at me. But I would have to cheat next time, and the next time and the next time. If I went back to only getting a few right, she would say that I hadn't bothered to learn them properly. Luckily it was near the end of Year 5, so I cheated every week and luckily I didn't get caught.

There was a horrible girl in my class called Margaret Sulky. She was the main reason that I didn't really have any friends. I didn't understand why, but she used to pick on me all the time. She was always saying nasty things. She would skit me about my reading, Call me things like 'Jenny no brain', and would tell the other children not to play with me because I had a brain problem which they could catch.

Once, when one of the girls was having a sleepover, she said to me in front of the others, "You're not invited on this sleepover because you wet the bed".

Some of the other children were nice but I think they were afraid of Margaret because she was big and looked older than her age, so they did what she said. When I couldn't do the work in class I sometimes used to cry and she always said things like, "Cry Baby". When she walked past me she used to say "baa aa, baa aa" like a sheep. This was because in our Christmas Concert Mrs. Old had given me the part of a sheep. I couldn't have a part which involved remembering lines or reading anything.

# 2

## THE SWIMMING TRIP

My worst memory of Year 5 happened when we were told that the whole class were going swimming on the last day of term, which was the following Friday. Our sports coach Mr. Runner and Miss Young were taking us. He told us that at the end of the lesson the good swimmers would have a race and the winner would get a cup.

I was really looking forward to it. I was really good at swimming, because my dad used to take me to the baths, and he taught me to swim properly. We used to have races, and I could beat him. He told me that I was a fantastic swimmer because nobody ever beat him. And I could dive. I even thought that I might win the cup. I didn't really mind if I didn't, as long as I was in the final.

I arrived at school with my swimming kit, feeling really excited. At last everyone would be able to see that I was good at something.

Miss Young told us that in the afternoon after the swimming, there would be a party and a Disco.

Before break we had a maths test, and then we were going to the baths, on a coach. After break we went to our classroom. Mrs. Old then announced that two children were not being allowed to go swimming, because they hadn't tried in the maths test. This would be a lesson for them.

"I don't mind if you can't do it. But there is no excuse for not even trying. The two children not going to the baths are . . . . Jenny Button and . . . ."

I didn't hear the other name. I felt like I had been punched in the stomach. I felt out of breath. The tears ran down my cheeks. I cried and cried.

On the way out of the class Margaret Sulky pulled a tongue and said, "Serves you right, Cry baby."

I made a rude sign at her with my fingers. She told Mrs. Old, who believed her, and shouted at me, 'You really are a naughty, nasty, little girl. You deserve to be missing the swimming trip.'

When I stopped crying I felt really angry. I decided that I was going to stand up to Margaret Sulky. I didn't even mind if I had a fight with her, and I didn't care if I lost. I planned it in my head. I would stand near her and stare. When she said something nasty to me, which was bound to happen, I would say something back. I decided that I would skit her name. My Nan has a friend called Margaret who is always called Madge. She once told me there are lots of ways that the name Margaret can be shortened: Madge, Marge, Maggie, Margie and Peggy. I also decided that whatever happened I wasn't going to cry. I didn't want Margaret to think she could make me cry.

When the class got back from the baths I heard that Margaret Sulky had won the swimming cup. This made me even more determined to stand up to her.

It all went to plan. We were all on the yard. I stood near Margaret and stared at her. Right away she growled. "What are you looking at loser?"

"I'm looking at you Madge," I replied.

"What did you call me?"

"I called you Madge, because it is short for Margaret. From now on I'm going to call you Madge and so is everyone else".

I couldn't stop grinning, and I noticed some of the other children were grinning as well. And then I added. "Unless you'd rather be called Marge, like Marge Simpson, because that's short for Margaret as well. Let me know what you want us to call you. Madge, Marge or maybe Peggy".

Margaret ran at me shouting, "I'll teach you to speak to me like that", and she pushed me hard in the chest. I pushed her back. Then she slapped me across the face. I slapped her back. She started crying, and ran towards the school door shouting, "I'm going to tell Mr. Pomp".

Mr. Pomp was the headmaster. A few minutes later he walked onto the yard and said firmly. "Jenny Button. I want to see you. Come with me."

He asked me to tell him what had happened. I told him that Margaret had started it, and that she had been bullying me and calling me names all year. I told him that my dad had told me that you should always stand up to bullies, so I had decided to do just that. He told me that Margaret had told him a different story. She told me that you had hit her for no reason, and she was very upset. He told me to sit on a chair in the school office, while he investigated the matter.

I thought I would be in big trouble. Mr. Pomp used to talk about bullying a lot in assemblies. He often told us about the school bullying policy. "If two children are fighting, they will both be in trouble. You cannot say that the other person started it. That's the excuse that bullies often use. If you are being bullied you must report it to a teacher. You must not start a fight".

I thought he would phone my mum and tell her to take me home.

After some time he came back and took me into his office. I waited for the bad news, but I couldn't believe what he said. "Sit down Jenny. I've spoken to two dinner ladies, and they have both told me that they saw what happened. Margaret started the trouble. They also told me that she has bullied you before. Therefore I am not taking any further action against you. But you must promise me that there will be no more fighting." I felt a huge wave of relief pass through my body. I felt like jumping up in the air and shouting "YESSSSSS."

He told me to sit on a chair outside his office, and then he went to get Margaret Sulky. They went into the office, and shut the door. I stood up and moved closer to the door, so I could listen to what he was saying. I could hear every word. I heard him say, "I have spoken to two dinner ladies and to several children about the incident. It is clear that you have been bullying Jenny Button. I spoke to the children separately and they have all told me the same story. I am phoning your mother to discuss the matter with her".

Margaret was crying and insisting that she hadn't done anything wrong. "They're all lying", she cried.

And it got better. That afternoon Mr. Pomp came to talk to the class. He talked about the school bullying policy, and why it was so important. He talked about different types of bullying. "Children have a right to come to school and feel safe. Bullying causes unhappiness and suffering. Victims of bullying have to live with fear and worry. Bullying spoils lives. No human being should want to cause suffering to another. It is wrong".

The whole class listened in complete silence.

He went on to explain that the bully also needs help. "Unless the bully is helped, they can't go on to have a normal life. There may be reasons for their behavior. They may have been bullied themselves."

He told the class he had found out that there had been serious bullying. "Jenny has been the victim." He said.

He told the class that they had all failed to do their duty. "Often the victim doesn't report the bullying because they are too frightened, or too nervous. They sometimes think they won't be believed or that nothing will happen and the bullying could get worse. This is why it is the duty of other children to report bullying", he stated.

He finished by thanking the three children who had been brave, and told him the truth about the incident on the yard. He said that there were a lot of children who should apologize to Jenny for doing nothing. "If you do not report bullying, you are part of the problem."

It was strange, but because I was so pleased with the way it worked out, for once I didn't feel ashamed being talked about in front of the class, and I had got over the disappointment of not being allowed to go swimming.

It got even better. Margaret Sulky didn't come back to class for the party. Lots of children spoke to me at the party, and said that they were sorry that they hadn't stuck up for me. Two girls, Amy Connor and Sophie Dean, who used to hang around with Margaret told me that they had told Mr. Pomp the truth. They said they were sorry for not doing anything before. They asked me to be friends with them and said that in future they would say something to Margaret if she was nasty to anyone. Sophie told me that she didn't really like Margaret. Two boys told me that they thought it was hilarious when I called Margaret, "Madge."

Before we went home I found out that our teacher in Year 6 was going to be Miss Young. She was really nice and kind.

I had the feeling that next year things were going to be better.

# 3

## THE SUMMER HOLIDAYS

I had a brilliant school summer holiday that year. We didn't go away, but I had lots of days out. I didn't have to worry about spelling tests, being asked to read, Mrs. Old telling me off or Margaret Sulky being nasty to me.

I still sometimes thought about my reading, and this still made me feel unhappy. Three people helped me to have a brilliant summer—My dad, my Nan and my best friend Kirsty.

I had always really loved my dad. My mum was strict and told me off a lot, but my dad was different. He used to take me out, and we always had fun together. He often took me swimming, and taught me to swim properly. He liked sporty things. When he took me out that summer, he said that Kirsty could come too. We went swimming a lot and he taught Kirsty to swim. Once we went to a pool in Wales with big slides and a wave machine. Afterwards he took us to the fairground. Another time he took me go-karting. At first I had to go on with him, but when I learnt to drive the go-kart, I was allowed to go on my own, if it was quiet.

My dad knew that I liked animals, so he took me and Kirsty to a Safari Park, and to a place called "Farm World", where you could feed the baby animals. He always bought us ice-creams and fizzy drinks.

One day, when the three of us were all having lunch in a Pizza restaurant, he amazed me by telling us that he was dyslexic as well as me. This was something that he hadn't told me before.

Kirsty looked surprised because I had never told her about my reading. And then, amazingly, Kirsty said that she was dyslexic as well, but she had had a lot of help. Her reading was now OK, but her spelling was still not that good.

My dad told me that I shouldn't worry about it. He said that he'd always had a job. He worked in a small factory which made wooden furniture. His boss had told him that he was the most skilled worker in the factory, and he got extra wages for training new workers. His boss had also told him that he thought that dyslexic people were usually very skilful.

He told us that when he is writing he often gets some of the letters of a word in the wrong place. He told us that he always gets mixed up with words which look like each other, like 'form' and 'from', and 'being' and 'begin'.

The next day Kirsty and I talked about our dyslexia. She told me that she only started to learn to read when she was eight. She was lucky, because her mum worked as a teaching assistant in her school, and she had been trained to work with dyslexic children. She became interested in the first place because she wanted to help Kirsty. Now her job was to help children who had trouble with reading, writing or maths. She said that her mum was really good at her job and was always getting thank-you cards from children or their mums. Kirsty told me that her mum knew lots of things you can do to help with reading, and that they practiced nearly every night. She told me that she can now read the Harry Potter books.

I told Kirsty about the terrible time I had at school, and how unhappy I felt because I couldn't read. I told her how I dreaded some lessons, and how I thought that there was something wrong with me. I told her that I tried to keep it a secret out of school. I hadn't told her about it because I thought she might not want to be friends with me if she knew. Kirsty started crying and gave me a hug. "I can ask my mum to help you", she said, "I know she will, because she loves her job".

"Yes please", I replied.

Kirsty and I had been friends since we were little. She was just like her mum.

They were both happy, friendly people who always seemed to be smiling. She never said anything nasty about anyone. When we were young, she got a bike before me, and she let me ride it loads of times. Kirsty's friendship was very important to me, because I didn't have a brother or sister, and I had no real friends at school.

Her house was a really happy house. Her mum and step-dad were always laughing and joking, and they never seemed to tell her off. And she was allowed to have a mobile phone.

During the holidays Kirsty's mum took her on lots of days out, and told her that she could take a friend with her. She always chose me. We went ice skating three times and we went to Alton Towers. We both liked going on scary rides. Her mum would come on the rides with us, but her step-dad was too chicken.

She would often let Kirsty choose a present for herself and would let me choose one as well.

Kirsty told her mum about my dyslexia. Her mum spoke to my mum and they agreed that she would help me with my reading. No time would be wasted. We would start the next day.

I enjoyed the lessons and improved quickly. We did lots of work using sounds. She would put letters on the table and ask me to make three letter words. When I made a word she then asked me to change a letter in my head. If I made the word 'hot' she would say, "what would it be if you changed the 'o' to an 'a.'" We then made four letter words. She also did lessons using my fingers to help me to see the way that letters go together to make words. "The most important part of a word is the vowel and letter after it".

I would hold up four fingers. She would put the two middle fingers together and say, "those fingers are 'a' and 'n'. Put them together and they make 'an'. Can you put a letter at the beginning and one at the end to make the word 'hand'".

We studied lots of words. I learnt to spell words by saying them slowly.

Kirsty's mum told me that she was amazed at how quickly I learnt. She then said, "I can tell that you have a good brain, and that you are a clever girl".

I was shocked. She said that I was clever. Nobody had ever told me that before. ME CLEVER! WOW! It felt wonderful. I couldn't stop smiling.

I started practicing reading books. I found that I was remembering words much better than before. I started to read the Wellington Square Reading Scheme, and soon I had read all the

Red books and had started on the
Green books. I had three weeks before
we went back to school. I decided to
practice like mad for these three weeks,
so that I could improve as much as I
could before the new term started.

The other person who helped me to
have a great summer was my Nan.
My Nan lived in the next street and
I had often stayed with her. I even
had my own bedroom in her house. I
loved staying there. She always called

me 'Pet'. I think it's because she's from Newcastle. She always had sweets or chocolate treats for me. She would let me stay up late, and would get DVDs that I liked. When I was younger she would play games with me like 'Snakes and Ladders', which I think is a bit boring now. She used to let me win.

She talked to me a lot. She often told me tales from when she was young. She was from a big family and they were very poor. She told me a story which I thought was sad, but she was laughing as if it was funny. "Once, my mam sent me to the butchers to ask for a bone for the dog, and then she used the bone to make soup for our dinner".

When I discussed my reading problems with my Nan, she smiled and said. "There's nothing to worry about Pet. Your granddad couldn't read and neither could his brother and they both worked in the shipyards and did really well in life. And your dad's never been much good at reading and writing and look at him. He's got a good job, a car, and he's buying a house. Your mother doesn't know how lucky she is to have him".

"It's better to be nice than clever", she often said. "Practice being nice and everything will be fine".

The holidays came to an end and as I got my school bag ready for Monday morning I couldn't help wishing that the holidays could last forever. "At least", I thought, "I'm not as worried as I was a year ago".

There are some good things. I am getting help with my reading and writing, and they're improving. I'm not scared of Margaret Sulky anymore. Amy and Sophie want to be friends with me. I've got Miss Young as my teacher.

# 4

## I LOVE SCHOOL

It was the first day of the new school
year, and as I walked slowly to school
I had the same feeling of dread in my
stomach. But it wasn't as bad as before.
There were some things to feel better
about. I had been working with Kirsty's

mum and my reading had improved. I was now reading 'Wellington Square Blue Books'. Miss Young was my class teacher and she was nice.

As I walked through the gates of the schoolyard, I heard a voice shout, "Hi Jenny".

Amy and Sophie ran across to me and gave me a hug. Some other children said 'hello', and they were all friendly.

Ben Smith told us that Margaret Sulky had left our school and was starting at a new one. He found out because his auntie knew Margaret's auntie. Margaret's mum said that she was taking her out the school because she was blamed for bullying and she hadn't done anything. He told us that Margaret's family had a lot of problems. Her dad was in prison, her older brother was always getting into trouble with the Police and her mum had to take tablets for her nerves.

I thought of Mr. Pomp's words. "Often, the bully needs help". I felt a bit sorry for Margaret, but I was still glad that she wasn't coming back. Amy and Sophie said that they were also pleased that she had left. Sophie said that she had been worried about telling Margaret she didn't want to be friends with her anymore.

At break on that first morning Miss Young asked me and two other children, Emily and Jack, to stay behind for a few minutes, so she could speak to us. She told us that we were going to get a lot of help with our reading and spelling. On Friday afternoon another teacher would take our class for French, and she would take the three of us for a literacy lesson. We would also work every day in a one-to-one with Miss Edwards, a Teaching Assistant.

When Friday came we went with Miss Young to another room. She talked to us about dyslexia and asked us how we felt about it. I told her that I hated being dyslexic and said, "I wish I could just press a button and I'd be clever".

Miss Young smiled and said, "but Jenny, there is no connection between reading and cleverness. Many dyslexic people are very clever and they are often very successful. A lot of scientists and engineers are dyslexic. I think you are clever. I can tell by your language skills. They're very good".

She patted me on the back and said, "don't worry Jenny, I think you're going to be a star".

She told us lots of things about dyslexia. She told us that she was very interested in it, and knew a lot about it. She said that lots of people have some dyslexia and that when she was young she did. She also told us that they now know a lot more about dyslexia, because there has been a lot of research using brain scanners. The scientists can tell which part of the brain a person is using when they read words. The dyslexic person is using a different part of the brain. They are not using the part of the brain that processes sounds.

"If you do lots of different phonic exercises and you practice using sounds to help you to read and spell words, then this part of your brain develops, and reading and spelling become easier".

The following Friday Miss Young gave the three of us a reading and a spelling test. She told me that I had improved since I was last tested just before the holidays. I felt really good and I told her about Kirsty's mum and the help I was getting. The lesson that week was fun. We wrote words on a sand tray using our fingers, and went on the yard and wrote words by squirting water. Miss Young said that every week she would talk to us about something that would help us to learn.

"I want you to understand something about achievement." She told us.

"Achievement is not the result of ability or talent. It comes from character and effort.

It is not the cleverest who are the best learners and who get the best results. It is those who work the hardest, and who never give up.

In life you make choices which have a big effect on your destiny. Choose not to be lazy. Laziness imprisons you in a cage surrounded by low expectations which can define your life. Don't let laziness prevent you from experiencing a life of growth and success, a life of confidence and self-belief. It's all about character. Great effort . . . . Great success."

I loved listening to Miss Young, and for the rest of the day her words were going around in my head. That evening I told

Kirsty the things Miss Young had said, and she thought they were brilliant as well. We both agreed that we would always try to make a great effort, and that we would never give up.

The next week Miss Young said that I would work with her on my own for some of the lesson because I had moved to a higher level than Jack and Emily. They would work with Miss Edwards and then we would swap over. This week she said that she wanted to talk to us about self esteem. She told us that children who are dyslexic nearly always have low self esteem, which leads to a lack of confidence. This can affect everything that you do. In life you need confidence.

She said that she had noticed that none of us put our hands up in class when she asked questions. I told her that I didn't put my hand up even if I knew the answer because I was too nervous. Jack and Emily said the same. She told us that when our reading improved we would become more confident, and would be happy to put our hands up. I decided that I would try to put my hand up sometime in the next week.

Miss Young then made me smile. She said that the best way of raising our self esteem was for a teacher to give us lots of praise. She turned to me and said, "Jenny, if I keep telling you that you are doing really well and that you are fantastic or brilliant or you are a star or other such things, you won't get fed up will you?"

I laughed and said "definitely not".

She smiled and asked me to promise. Then she said the same to Jack and Emily.

The next day I put my hand up in class for the first time. It was in a history lesson. Miss Young was talking about the Romans, and she asked us to think about what the Romans thought when they first arrived in Britain. I put my hand up and she immediately said "Yes Jenny".

I could feel everyone looking at me. "Miss", I answered, "they probably thought that it was cold".

"That's an excellent answer Jenny", she said, "and one of the things we are going to learn is how the Romans heated their villas".

I couldn't help thinking how different Miss Young was to Mrs. Old.

For the next few weeks I did reading and spelling every day with Miss Edwards, I went to Miss Young every Friday, and I worked with Kirsty's mum twice a week. On the other nights I practiced on my own and with my mum. I finished the yellow level of Wellington Square. Miss Edwards told me that I was ready to read some proper books. We read a book called 'Living with Vampires' which was funny. She then gave me a book to read at home called 'Betrayal', which was about the friendship of two girls in Nazi Germany. One of the girls was Jewish and the other one was German. Once I'd started the book, I couldn't put it down. I was enjoying it so much. This had never happened to me before. "Gosh", I thought, "I love reading".

Kirsty told me that she had lots of books and that I could borrow them.

I was also starting to do much better in other lessons. Miss Young showed me a good way of learning tables. She said that children who are dyslexic nearly always have trouble remembering their tables. I practiced at home and started to remember them.

Once a week in class we would have 'Circle Time'. I used to love this lesson. Our chairs were all arranged in a circle and Miss Young would talk about different things which she said was to help us to grow into quality people. She told the class some of the things she had told Jack, Emily and me in our literacy lesson. One week it was all about making choices which make your life better. She talked about the choice to always make a great effort, and the choice not to be lazy. I loved hearing it again. One week she told me that she would like to talk about dyslexia and would like to mention me, but only if I agreed. I did.

She told the class about dyslexia and how it affects children. She said that we have some children in our class who are dyslexic. She said. "Jenny is dyslexic. She has a good brain and is actually a clever girl. But when a child is younger they don't understand this. They think there is something wrong with them. They have a very hard time at school. They are often very unhappy. They worry a lot. Sometimes they are picked on by other children. They need help with their work and they need other children to be kind, but often this doesn't happen".

Amy looked at me and started crying. I also noticed that Sophie was crying. When the lesson was over they both gave me a hug and Amy said that she wished that she had helped me more.

Every month there was an assembly, where one pupil in each class got the pupil of the month award, and won a prize. Each class teacher would say who got the prize and why. Miss Young stood up and said, "The Class 6 prize goes to a pupil who has made amazing progress, who always works very hard, and is also a very nice, thoughtful and kind girl. Jenny Button". I nearly fell off my chair I was so surprised. I never won prizes.

As I walked up to get my prize I could feel a warm glow through my whole body. Everyone was clapping and cheering. Something like this had never happened to me before. All the teachers smiled at me as I walked past them, except one. When I got back to my place Amy was crying, and said, "I'm crying because I'm happy".

The next night was Parents Evening. My mum and dad went to the school, and I stayed with my Nan. When they got back my mum gave me a hug and told me that Miss Young had given me a brilliant report. She said that she would get me a mobile phone for

Christmas, as a reward. My Nan said that she would pay for me to have my hair and nails done at the hairdressers.

Over the next few weeks Year 6 got the chance to visit the secondary schools they could go to. My mum wanted me to go to 'Our Lady's High School for Girls', which was quite near and she had heard good things about it. Nearly all the girls in my class went to an evening at Our Lady's. I was with my mum and dad. So was Sophie, but Amy was just with her mum because she doesn't have a dad. We met all the teachers and they seemed to be really nice. We met a teacher called Miss Copewell who was the SENCO. She told the parents that the school gave help to any pupil who needed it with literacy or numeracy. She said that they had helped a lot of children in the past who had gone on to do well. One girl who had been dyslexic in Year 7 was now at university training to be a teacher. She told my mum that I would get help.

I wanted to go to Our Lady's and the next day I was really happy when I heard that Amy and Sophie were going there as well. I couldn't believe it when I heard a few days later that Kirsty was going to Our Lady's too.

I lay in bed that night thinking how much everything had changed in such a short time. As I drifted off to sleep I thought of Miss Young's words.

**"Great Effort. Great Success"**

Lightning Source UK Ltd.
Milton Keynes UK
UKOW050508160812

197616UK00001B/23/P